HENRY THE STEINWAY
A STAR IS BORN

By Sally Coveleskie and Peter Goodrich   ❖   Illustrated by Laura Friedman

For the men and women of Steinway & Sons
S.C. & P.G.

For my parents
L.F.

Special thanks to the staff of New York's incomparable Carnegie Hall

Heartfelt appreciation to our family and friends, Ana, Gerhard, Tim, Veronica, and Vince,
for their love and encouragement, and to our editor, Kate

Our gratitude to music consultant James McVoy

YORKVILLE
PRESS

Text copyright © 2003 by Sally Coveleskie and Peter Goodrich
Illustrations copyright © 2003 by Laura Friedman

Library of Congress Cataloging-in-Publication Data

Coveleskie, Sally,
Henry the Steinway : a star is born / Sally Coveleskie and Peter Goodrich ;
illustrations by Laura Friedman.
p. cm.
Summary: Describes how Henry the Steinway was built, his life as a concert piano,
and how he came to live in the house of a girl named Ana.
ISBN 0-9729427-1-8
[1. Piano—Fiction.]
I. Goodrich, Peter, II. Friedman, Laura, ill. III. Title.

PZ7.C8339He 2003
[E]—dc21

2003007163

Book and jacket design by Kathryn W. Plosica
Printed in Hong Kong through Asia Pacific Offset

jes 10 9 8 7 6 5 4 3 2 1

It was a beautiful, crisp fall day! Ana watched the children outside her window hurry to school. She wished she could join them.

"Oh! What a terrible cold! I can't believe I'm sniffling and sneezing and stuck in bed!" Ana said.

Ana sipped her juice and tried to stay warm under her cozy covers.

After reading some of her favorite books, Ana wanted a little company. She wrapped a blanket around her shoulders and wandered down the hall to the music room. There she heard the familiar voice of her best friend, Henry the Steinway.

"Hello, Ana. I'm so glad you're out of bed. Why don't we play some music together? It will make you feel better."

Ana and Henry began to play together just like they did every day. After a few measures, Ana forgot all about her sniffles!

"Henry, I really do feel better!" she said.

Ana was so busy playing with Henry that she didn't notice her father coming through the doorway with her two dogs, Emma and Molly. They were happy to see that Ana was perking up!

"Here, Ana, have some tea with honey, and then let's play our famous father-daughter duet."

Playing music with her father always made Ana feel happy. Henry smiled as he felt their fingers march across his keys.

Then, something very strange happened. One of Henry's keys went down and it would not come back up again. Ana and her father pressed the key over and over, but it would not bounce back.

"Ana, I think the only one who can help Henry now is Mr. Ron, the piano tuner," said Father. "Don't worry. Sometimes pianos feel out of sorts just like people do. I'll call Mr. Ron and ask him to come over and examine Henry right away."

"Henry must have a cold, too," thought Ana. So she wrapped him in a soft blanket to keep him warm while they waited.

When Mr. Ron arrived, he sat on the bench and played Henry's keys. Then, he pulled Henry's keyboard all the way out and put it on his lap. Henry's keys had thousands of wooden pieces attached to them. At the end of each one were little hammers with round, fuzzy heads.

"What is this? What are all these? Is this how Henry works?" Ana asked in amazement.

"Yes, Ana," explained Mr. Ron, "Henry plays music because his many parts work well together. Each one has a special job to do. This part, for example, is called the action, and the little hammers strike Henry's strings to make a sound. These hammers were made at the Steinway piano factory where Henry was created. Would you like to come and see the factory sometime?" asked Mr. Ron.

"Yes… as soon as I'm all better," said Ana.

Mr. Ron finished fixing Henry's keys and put him back together.

"Good as new!" said the piano tuner.

"Good as new!" echoed Ana.

With that announcement, Henry played his keys up and down to show off how well they worked.

At her next lesson, Ana asked her teacher, Miss Yuriko, if the piano students could go to the Steinway piano factory.

"What a wonderful idea!" said Miss Yuriko.

The following week, the children boarded a bright yellow bus for their special outing. When they arrived, Manager Mike greeted them. "Welcome to the Steinway factory, children. Let's go see where Henry was made."

Ana and her friends — Lily, Alec and Buzzy — followed Manager Mike to the lumberyard where huge stacks of wood were drying in the sun. He explained that pianos are made mostly of wood that comes from different types of trees grown all over the world.

"How long does this wood dry in the lumberyard?" asked Buzzy.

HOOL BUS   6851

"Good question," said Manager Mike. "This wood stays here for at least one whole year before it is ready to be made into a piano."

"After the wood is selected and dried, it is cut into long planks. We put them into a rim press and bend them into Henry's familiar frame."

"Is that what gives him his graceful curve?" asked Lily.

"Yes," said Manager Mike. "Henry's grand piano shape is made in the rim press."

Lily and Buzzy really liked what they saw next. "What's this?" they asked Manager Mike.

"This part is called the soundboard, and it's the heart and soul of the piano. Because of it, Henry can roar as loud as a lion or sing as sweetly as a nightingale.

"See those sturdy iron plates over there? Henry's strings stretch across them when he finally becomes a piano," replied Manager Mike.

"Let's go down the hall to the action department," suggested Manager Mike. "There you can see how we craft the parts of the piano that make Henry's keys go up and down. It's also the place where Henry's hammers were made."

"How many keys are there on the piano?" Manager Mike asked.

The children answered together, "There are 88!"

"How many black ones?" Manager Mike asked with a twinkle in his eye. And before anyone had time to count them, he told them there are 36!

The action maker gave each of the children a sample hammer to take home. "These hammers look a lot different than the ones in my uncle's toolbox," observed Alec.

"Now, our last stop on the tour is a visit to the polishing department. This is where Henry got his sleek, black finish. After this final step, a special number is stamped onto the piano's plate," Manager Mike said, as they watched while the serial number was applied to a new piano: 5 3 6 5 9 3.

Then the tour was over, and Miss Yuriko and the children shook hands with Manager Mike and said good-bye to all the people they had met in the factory.

"Thank you for showing us how Henry was made," they said as they boarded the bus.

When she got home, Ana changed out of her school clothes and ran to the music room.

"Henry, I had so much fun learning about you in the factory. Now, I know all of your parts. Maybe I'll work in the piano factory someday," said Ana as she tapped him with the fuzzy hammer.

"Maybe you will," said Henry. "It seems like such a long time ago when I said good-bye to all the workers there."

"Is that when you came to my house?" Ana asked.

"Well, I made a few stops along the way," recalled Henry.

My journey to your house started on the day I left the factory. My best friend, Pianissimo, and I were completed on the same day. She was a beautiful art case piano, very different from me. I was just a plain, black grand piano.

Together we were carefully loaded onto the delivery truck.

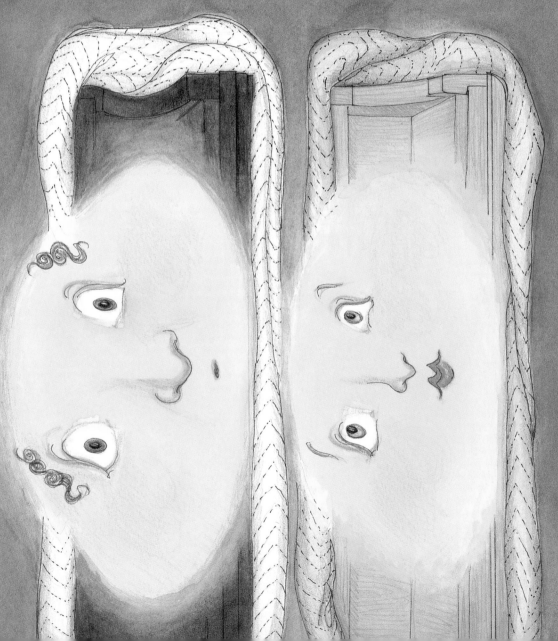

"Where do you think we're going?" Pianissimo asked me.

"We could be sent anywhere in the world," I answered. "You are so beautiful, Pianissimo, perhaps you will live in a palace or even the White House. I am not so sure about my new home. Maybe I will be sent to a music school. If I am, I hope the students will take good care of me."

The truck finally arrived at its destination: Steinway Hall in New York City. The piano movers placed Pianissimo in the building's most elegant salon. She looked so glamorous under the glow of the glittering chandeliers.

The movers put me on a big elevator and I went all the way downstairs! At first, it seemed that no one paid much attention to me. It was very busy there. I had never seen so many concert grand pianos like me in one place! Then I realized I must be in the famous Steinway Concert Basement.

Pianists from all over the world came to the basement to choose a piano for their important performances. Though we were all concert grand pianos, there was something special about the sound and feel of each one of us.

Some pianos were chosen for jazz concerts, some for rock, while others were chosen espe-

cially for classical music. There was a piano for EVERY kind of music, and each of us wanted to be selected. We all wondered, "Who will choose me?"

I was brand new. It was my very first day at work. I stood in a straight line with the other pianos, waiting to be chosen.

At first, I was passed over by many pianists who would go straight to their old favorites. But then I began to be chosen for concerts in many different places: from big cathedrals to jazz clubs to opera

houses, even to TV studios! I was going out so often, that the other pianos whispered to each other, "There must be something special about Henry!"

One day I'll always remember… There was quite a 'hum' in the air. Mr. Ron took me to his workbench and gave me a very thorough physical. He poked and filed my hammers, straightened and tightened my action, brushed off my soundboard, and finally, tuned me so beautifully that I felt I could fly. The polisher buffed out my rim, and I sparkled like a patent leather shoe.

"Where in the world could I be going?" I asked Mr. Ron. With a great big smile, he told me that the Carnegie Hall Steinway was going to be retired, and I was chosen to take her place!

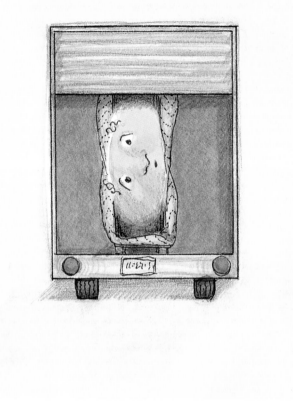

As I rode along in the delivery truck, I asked myself,

"Am I brave enough?"
"Am I strong enough?"
"Can I do it?"

When I arrived backstage, there she was – the Carnegie Hall Steinway! Over many years of faithful service, she had proven herself to be both brave enough and strong enough. Maybe I could do it after all!

"Henry," she whispered, "I have had a wonderful career here. I have played together with the great pianists of the world, and for many years our music has filled this famous place.
Now, my concert days have come to an end. I have always hoped to live someday with a real family, and today my dream is coming true. I look forward to where I am going next.

"I know you will have a great future here in Carnegie Hall, Henry. Play well."

She then said good-bye and was gently moved from the stage for the very last time.

There I was, all alone on the vast stage. The house lights dimmed, and I felt the warmth of a bright spotlight on my face. My career as the Carnegie Hall Steinway was about to begin, and I had a feeling it was going to be glorious!

I became known as the greatest piano of them all. I worked with the most famous pianists in the world, but your father was always my favorite. We played many beautiful recitals together. One day, after a very special performance, he whispered to me,

"Henry the Steinway, you are my best friend. Someday you will come to live with me, and we will always play together."

"And, so it was, dear Ana," said Henry. "When it was my turn to leave Carnegie Hall, I came to live here. That was the happiest day of my life. Now, you and I can play beautiful music, and we'll always be together, too!"

That night, as Ana slept, she dreamed that she and Henry were playing together at Carnegie Hall. When the audience applauded their performance, Ana whispered to Henry, just as her father once did,

"Henry the Steinway, you are my best friend."

And she gave him a little kiss... right above Middle C.